To my very own apples
Miss Courtney Clay
Miss Claire Morgan
Miss Chloe Elizabeth &
Miss Charley Anne
With Love

First published 2011 by Gardner Media LLC • 71 South Orange Ave., South Orange, NJ 07079 • gardnerpub@aol.com
Concept and illustration © Ellen Brenner Sørensen 2011 • Text © Paul J. Gardner 2011 • All rights reserved
ISBN 978-1-936979-08-0 • CLP042511GDAP06019080 • Printed and bound in Shenzhen, China

Grandy Apple

Created by Ellen Brenner-Sørensen

Written by Joe Gardner   Illustrated by Alessandra Gasparini

Gardner Publishing

South Orange, NJ

This is my Grandy,
Grandy Apple,
Grandest Apple in the World.

"Hello,
my sweet little fruits!"

Candy Apple
is my Mom.
Candy
Apple
Candy
Apple

Caramel Apple is my Dad.
My Dad is Caramel Apple.

I am Hannah.
I am a Banana.
I am the Biggest
And the Oldest
And the Biggest.

These are my sisters,
My younger sisters.
Polly is a Pineapple,
and
Penny is a Pear.

We live
We live
in an
Apple Orchard.
Grandy and Candy,
Caramel, Polly, Penny
And Me

We live in
an Apple Orchard.

Squish, squish
Squash, squash
Working hard
Working hard
Squish, squish
Squash, squash
Making Apple Cider

We make Apple Cider for the villages all around.

There is much to do,
but Grandy says
make sure you stop
every now and then,
take a breath,
and be grateful.

She takes us to school and picks us up again. "Isn't this fun?" she says.

In the summer,
she takes us to the beach,
to the beach.
"Isn't this fun? she says,
Isn't this fun?"

We play on the Beach.
Every day
Every day
Polly has a new bikini.
Penny brings her snorkel.

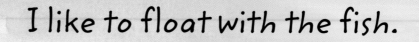

I like to float with the fish.

On Grandy's birthday,
every year,
we have a Party.
A Big Party

We dress up,
dress up

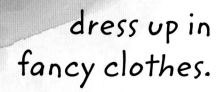

dress up in
fancy clothes.

Grandy Apple, Grandy Apple
Grandest Apple
in the World

has the
Grandest Dress.

Candy Apple
is so pretty.
Candy Apple
is so pretty.

Caramel
is handsome.
Caramel
is dashing.

We love to dress
To dress up
To dress up

Polly the Pineapple
Penny the Pear
and Me
and Me
Hannah the Banana.

Happy Birthday
We sing
Happy Birthday
To Grandy,
Grandy Apple.
Candy, and Caramel
Polly and Penny
and Me
sing

Happy Birthday
Happy Birthday
Happy Birthday dear Grandy

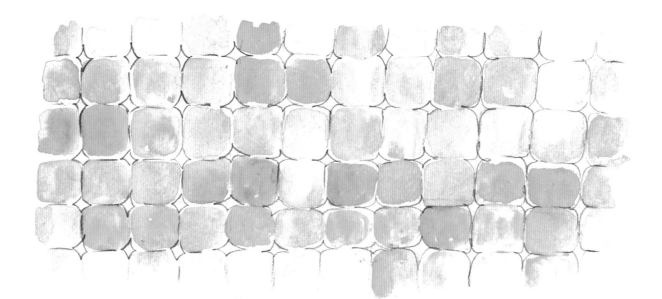

After the party
When the party is over
We take a Bath,
a Bath,
a long, hot Bath.
Grandy tells us stories.
We tell stories to her.

Then we go to Bed, Go to Bed. Go to Bed.
Grandy kisses us, each one of us,
and says "I love you,
each one of you,
my sweet little fruits."

And we say,
"We love you, Grandy
Apple. We love you, too."